A

LOVE

LIKE

TEXAS WEATHER

FEHMI NUHOGLU

AUSTIN, TEXAS

For permission requests, e–mail the publisher with the e–mail addressed to "Permissions Coordinator,"

For all other inquiries, comments, questions, new ideas, or write to the author, please use the "Contact Us" page at:

www.round–rock–records.com

Ordering Information: Quantity sales. Special discounts are available on quantity purchases by corporations, associations, and others. For details, contact the "Special Sales Department" through the website above.

This is a work of fiction. Names, characters, places, and incidents either are the product of the author's imagination or are used fictitiously, any resemblance to actual persons, living or dead, businesses, companies, events, or locales is entirely coincidental.

Editing: WritingTexan.com & Inksnatcher.com
Book Layout: BookDesignTemplates.com
Book Cover Design: Dick Reeves Design
Author's Photo: Emre Ogan – www.ogan.com

A Love Like Texas Weather / Fehmi Nuhoglu
ISBN–13: 978–1–5429–46643
ISBN–10: 1–5429–4664–6
e–ISBN–13: 978–0–692–84701–5
e–ISBN–10: 0–692–84701–4

CONTENTS

For Irem, my wife and my rock,

and

for Eda, my daughter and my pride

"Austin, Texas is a deep source of inspiration
with its diversity in music, unique lifestyle, and tranquility"

— FEHMI NUHOGLU aka FRANKY

THE BEGINNING

Travis is born with his name written in his eyes, which are the color of a beloved childhood memory of his mother's: the waters of Lake Travis. An only child, his Austinite mother marries a country man and moves with him to a small Hill Country town.

Mom is happy enough on their small ranch, filled with Texas grasses and trees that roll up and down again like a lullaby and a creek that rarely runs dry, but she has never forgotten Austin. She sometimes regrets having left. Every night, while putting her little boy to bed, she tells him stories of its beauty. He falls asleep listening to her sweet voice singing, "Austin Holds a Place for Those Who Pray."

Dad, on the other hand, is pure cowboy, his days occupied with animals. He has a reputation as the best horse trainer and dressage master in a hundred-mile radius, and he's earned it. A tall man, broad-chested, with a Texan jawline, he has a way of staring into a horse's eyes and just knowing what that horse needs. He's tried to do the same to Travis—he sees Travis taking the reins of the ranch someday, so there has never been time in his son's life for any distractions: school and horses day and night, and that's all.

Taken up with caring for the horses day and night, neither of his parents knows that Travis has his own dreams. All his life, his grandfather's guitar sat on the mantle above the fireplace, a reminder of his mother's beloved dad—gone before Travis was born. From the age of ten, though, Travis takes every opportunity to slip the guitar from its sacred spot and run off to the barn. The old guitar wobbles at first on his small lap and many times refuses to respond to Travis's awkwardly placed finger sequences on the strings, but Travis slowly learns to play by ear, even figuring out how to tune the guitar himself. For years, the horses are his only audience, and they barely give him a glance. But slowly, passion has become ambition ... and an old guitar that never truly sings isn't going to be enough.

That means asking for his parents' help. *Dad would never get it, but Mom?* Well, she knows about regrets and dreams.

"Got something to show you, Mom," he says, pulling down the old six string. "I've been messing around with Granddad's guitar for a while now. Dad doesn't know, but the horses think I'm pretty good!" His heart is thumping faster than he's used to, but he breathes in and starts the chords of a simple song, singing the first few bars. His mother bursts into tears.

Confused, he stops. "Did I do something wrong?"

"Oh, Travis." She wipes at her eyes with the heel of her hand. "You sound just like my daddy when you play. I wish you could have known him!" Mom doesn't wait another minute. The old guitar goes back on the mantle, and she leaves a note for Dad on the counter:

Got some errands in the city. Back tonight with BBQ!

They get straight in the car and drive to Austin.

The salesman brings a few acoustic guitars over to the young musician—black and shiny, dark wood, lighter wood, guitars with recognized brand names—but all Travis cares about is the sound. Will it sing to his future audiences? He finally settles on a

Seagull with a wild cherry back and sides and a sound that strangely takes his mother back to her fading memories of Lake Travis.

"It's the best gift ever!" Travis runs his fingers over the wood in wonder. "But what are we going to tell Dad?"

"You just leave him to me."

For days, Travis waits for some comment from Dad, but his dad never brings up the subject. Dad knows better than to argue with Mom once her mind is made up (and besides, the guitar is already paid for). Still, his face tells Travis that nothing else has changed.

Horses are Travis's job, and he likes them okay, but despite their strength and graceful movements in the dressage ring, it's music he really loves. High school's a bore, which is clear from his grades. Dad doesn't much mind as long as he passes, because a cowboy doesn't need straight A's. All diplomas look the same to the rich folks and their purebred mares. Nobody in Dad's world is going to care about his son's GPA. Mom, however, quietly grieves as she watches her only son's chance at college slip away. She has always dreamed of more opportunities for her son than she was given. So—so grades mean no chance of a scholarship, and the family doesn't have the money for tuition at a place like the University of Texas.

Travis definitely wants to wind up in Austin, but he has his own plan for getting there. He and Dad go there each year for the Austin Rodeo, where they show clients' horses in dressage and roping. Every time, Travis has listened to the music that makes its way around the animal pavilions, where he mucks out stalls and brushes coats. When Dad leaves to drink beer and talk shop with old friends, Travis slips away to fill his ears with more of its riffs and beats. Rock, country, blues—he loves it all. He walks past the statues of Stevie Ray Vaughan and Willie Nelson, hangs around outside the bars on Sixth Street, or goes to Stubbs and stares at the pictures of famous Texan players. At night, on his own, he wanders and dreams. "They respect music here," he tells himself. "Nobody here laughs if you say you want to be an artist. This is the right place for me. And music is the right life."

Back home after each rodeo, Travis bides his time. He does what Mom and Dad tell him. He fills out the college applications, runs horses around barrels, and shows up on time for every class. But every moment he can get alone, he plays that new guitar. Finally, Travis graduates—barely—but he feels the freedom of the moment when he throws his hat in the air with his fellow classmates.

He's not surprised when UT rejects his application. Dad doesn't mind, which is no surprise, and it's okay by Travis, too, but it hurts to see Mom walk around the house with such a downcast face for weeks. The boy is relieved when her old friend Ed, a professor at the music school, sends a note:

> Travis is a good kid, Irene. Give him time to find himself and maybe one day he'll apply again. Send him over to visit me at the school the next time he's in town for the rodeo.

It seems to cheer her up (or at least quieten her down), so now he just has to deal with Dad's plans for his future.

Besides learning guitar–playing techniques from the internet and practicing them, he keeps helping on the ranch with no complaint. He was never one to shirk the hard work that goes into supporting the family. He starts to write songs for his mother, and his passion for music that floods the soul makes her happy. He figures he doesn't have to tell her his other motive—his dreams of making his life about so much more than horse hoofs on sand. Travis is working also on developing his own musical style.

What made guys like Stevie Ray and Willie so special? Their musical expression was completely unique to themselves, but they both wrote their own songs and loved Austin. Travis figures if he can find his unique style, he can go as far as they did. So in whatever time he finds to be alone, Travis writes. Day or night, sometimes without sleeping, Travis works on songs—humming, scratching out lines, reworking notes. His mother's smile grows, and his skills quickly mature.

Travis never forgets that Mom and the horses aren't his true audience. He has a bigger crowd in mind for his first performance: the Austin Rodeo. It's perfect. He attends every year. His father's friends on the organizing committee know him well. He just has to pick his moment—one when Dad is *not* around.

It is a wish that takes planning, one that could take a year or more to play out. But Travis knows how to be patient; he's been practicing the realization of his dream almost since he was born. First, he sends the music coordinator a letter:

Dave,

Looking forward to seeing you next month! Drop by the horse pavilion for a beer if you have time (not that you ever do). Listen, while we're in town, can I ask you to do me a favor? My kid has a new hobby—playing guitar. Mind letting him play a few of his songs and giving him some musical advice?

I'd love to see him perform at the rodeo some-day!

Sincerely

Travis mastered Dad's signature a long time ago, since he often has to sign for packages at the ranch. It's barely legible anyway, so he just had to figure out how to get the squiggles and the lines. It's easy to scratch it at the bottom of this letter. He feels the gnarly wriggle of guilt as he licks the envelope, but he gets over it quickly and sends it off...

...and checks the mailbox each day for a reply. Finally, a letter with the right return address arrives. Travis tears it open at the box while standing in the dirt road at the entrance to the ranch. He reads:

Happy to help. Send him over. No promises, though! And we will have that beer... after I retire maybe.

Dave

Travis whoops and jumps. "Yahoo!" He feels like he could jump high enough to touch those clouds up there. In the next moment, though, the guilt of his lie sets in. He has heard his dad say it a million times: "A cowboy is always happy to help an old friend." And now he tells himself, "It's not like I hurt any-body. It's just so I can play him my songs." If Dave doesn't like his music, that will be the end of it. If he does ... well, Dad will come around.

The days until the next rodeo seem to crawl by, but Travis and his dad eventually load up the trailer and head east. He wrangles the horses like always, listens to the bands, and waits for his moment. Finally, Dad heads off to look at the competition and Travis slips away.

Dave leans back into the chair in his trailer and listens to Travis play.

"That's some mighty fine joy you got there in those songs, son." He pats Travis on the back and says, "We'll be in touch."

Those words are not much to hang your hopes on, but Travis believes in the power of his dream. So when they get back to the ranch, he waits. He spends his days in the stables and his nights with the guitar. He writes songs. He does chores. He rides. The days turn into months. Travis waits and he dreams.

Finally, the next spring, a new letter arrives—this time, with his name on the front. On the dirt road down from the house, he tears the envelope in two, heart pounding. This year's king of the rodeo, a wealthy Austinite with some creative ideas, wants to sponsor an opening day parade. Dave has a spot for Travis playing on one of the floats. It's not a spot on one of the stages, but it's a start. How does that sound?

It sounds like fame calling! Playing on a float at the opening parade? Who could ask for more?

Travis runs the whole way home, his beat–up roper boots kicking up dust. "I'm gonna play the rodeo next year!" he shouts to his mom. Grabbing her in his arms, they two–step around the living room.

"Help me, Mom," he begs. "You've gotta talk Dad into letting me play."

"That's amazing, Travis," says Irene, "But how did they hear your songs?"

"Played them for Dave last year," he replies, keeping the rhythm of the dance.

"Dave? What did your dad say when he saw you?"

Travis slows to a waltz, "Well, Mom ... about that.... I went to Dave's office on my own. I thought Dad might get kinda mad if I told him...."

Mom stops in the middle of the living room and pulls away from her son. "Travis, are you telling me you lied to your daddy?"

What can he say? She always knows when he doesn't speak the truth. She always has. "I guess I did. I didn't tell him I was going to audition and I haven't said anything to him about it since. But, Mom, I really want to play. Can't you help me talk to him?"

"You don't give your dad enough credit," she sighs, "He's got a big heart. I'll talk to him, but you've got to promise me you won't do anything this sneaky again."

"I swear, Mom," replies Travis, sincerity shining in his lake blue eyes.

When Mom pulls his dad aside after dinner to tell him what Travis did, he says nothing. The next day, she promises Travis that everything will work out.

"Dad's agreed that you should play. And you should practice at every opportunity you get; just try not to leave all your chores undone. And Travis, he may not say it, but I can tell he's proud."

[1]

AUSTIN, I'M FLYING

If Travis thought time went slowly while he was waiting for the last letter, now he thinks it must have stopped altogether. It feels like years pass between the invitation and rodeo day. He tries to fill up the days with busywork, and there's certainly plenty to do around the ranch between mucking out stalls, hauling hay, exercising the horses, cleaning tack, trail clearing, and fixing fences.

The night before the rodeo finally arrives, Travis is sitting in the kitchen quieter than his mom has ever seen him. She's drying dishes and dinner pots, but she puts her dishcloth on the table for a moment and places a hand softly on his shoulder. "You nervous, hon?"

Travis puts his own hand up to hers. "Excited mostly," Travis insists. But he inhales sharply and admits, "I really want you both to be proud."

Mom squeezes his hand. "You've spent more time rehearsing than eating, sleeping, or working the horses put together. I think you're ready. And I know the animals are ready to stop hearing those songs over and over!"

"Damn right!" Dad laughs from the next room.

"You hush," Mom calls, "You want Travis to think you're not behind him?"

"I gave him time off all those chores, didn't I? And don't think I don't know you've been sneaking that guitar into the barn every day."

He knows his parents are nervous, too, and that the jokes are just a way of making the night less long. But when he puts his hands back under the table, Travis feels them tremble. He stands and slips outside.

It's a clear night with a half–moon casting damp shadows through the trees. Looking up at the sky, he thinks, *I'll be up there with those stars someday. Someday soon, too!*

But his gut isn't buying his brain's bull. Its voice is sharp, mean. "You've never been in front of a crowd before," it says. "You're shaking up a storm out here. You excited or just plain scared?"

Travis isn't sure whether he's strictly happy or not, but he knows one thing: he can't wait until he

stands on that stage and starts to sing. Gazing into
the inky blackness around the moon and stars, a sudden feeling of weightlessness overtakes him. His feet
feel light in his beat–up leather boots, almost like he's
walking among the clouds. He spreads his arms,
ready to fly, and sings:

> *Tonight, it's gonna be a long long night, tonight*
> *So light, I feel I'm floating, on a cloud*
> *With my feet, off the ground*
> *Austin, on my mind*
>
> *My life, I spent my whole life, to be a star*
> *My heart, thanks for keeping up, so far*
> *Endless days, nights too dark*
> *It was hard, how I tried*
>
> *My lord, can't beat that feeling, inside*
> *I'm scared, how I'm gonna face, the crowds*
> *With my hands, a–shaking*
> *With my feet, trembling*
>
> *I know*
> *It's my turn*
> *To make you all proud*
> *Proud of me*
>
> *I'm coming Austin*

And I' m flying

I'm flying, "I'm coming Austin"
I'm flying
I'm flying, "Austin, my dream"
I'm flying
I'm flying, "wait for me Austin"

[2]

AUSTIN RODEO

For years, die–hard rodeo fans have complained about how events like Austin City Limits and SXSW have stolen the rodeo's spotlight. This year's rodeo king, an incredibly rich local businessman, has sworn to change all of that. He has promised a return to the glory days, and looking at all the people wandering down Congress Avenue, Travis thinks he might pull it off. The rodeo king has spared no expense—funding new pavilions, a huge VIP party with celebrities, and bringing in performers from all over the world.

The opening parade is going to be insane: hundreds of cowboys, thousands of livestock, live music on moving stages. More astounding, the rodeo king convinced the mayor to extend the parade route over the Congress Avenue bridge.

It's going to be a rodeo to remember. Travis can hardly believe his luck.

> *Rodeo, Rodeo*
> *Welcome to Rodeo*
>
> *It's Austin city here, all is weird*
> *You just let yourself go*

Standing idly by his assigned float, Travis looks down the long, long line of Congress Avenue. TV cameras and microphones flash in the sun as far as the eye can see. All of the major stations are broadcasting live. "I could be performing for millions!" Travis thinks, feeling a thrill in his gut.

On the south side of the bridge, he can just see Bevo the Longhorn at the top of the parade column. The cheering crowds are throwing the UT hand sign and shouting: "Hook 'em Horns!" Travis can see that Austinites love that bull, as everybody lines up to get a picture with him.

Dave pulled some strings and got Travis on the very first music float, a huge moving platform decorated with a western theme—which he thinks is just a little cheesy—and equipped with loudspeakers. Travis will be leading the parade with his music. Two very important TV personalities are also riding with him, and he can see they've already begun their coverage.

Travis looks southward where the ranch riders are lining up. It looks like every major ranch in Texas is represented; he can see the flags waving and recognizes many of the brands. The cowboys are settling horses and adjusting their best Stetsons. What a beautiful sight!

Wow! There are so many of them. From the biggest one to the smallest outfits in Texas, it looks like all the ranches sent some representation. *Look at that!* Travis notices with surprise; *the biggest group is being led by a cowgirl!* The flag says "Rancho Austinado," but he doesn't look at it for long. Travis's eyes fix on the girl's long golden hair, strands of it dancing around her heart–shaped face. She's mounted on a beautiful white filly, balancing the flag on one trim thigh. If Travis was looking around, he'd see that many eyes are on her, but like them, he just stares at her. Maybe he can get a better look if he stands on top of the float. It's about time for the parade to start anyway.

He swings up onto the platform, careful of his new guitar. Now, the sheer size of the parade distracts him from the pretty cowgirl. It's huge. Beyond huge. He's a bit higher above the crowd, and he looks behind the cavalry. Travis can just make out the burnt orange of the UT Longhorn Marching Band. The shiny horns and drums flash as the marchers warm up. Suddenly Travis gets the layout. The organizers have it timed perfectly so the audience never has to be without music.

He plugs in his amp and stands with his guitar ready. He can just see the King of the Rodeo in the very front. The king raises his hat. The cowboys mount up and Travis puts his hands on the strings. He feels his float lurch into motion. Here we go, it's time for the show.

> *Rodeo, Rodeo*
> *Austin Rodeo*
>
> *It's Austin city here, all is weird*
> *You just let yourself go*
>
> *Rodeo, Rodeo*
> *Austin Rodeo*
>
> *It's Austin city here, all is weird*
> *You just let yourself go*

Roping cattle, bucking bronco
It's time for the show
Put on your chaps, get on your horse
Hold on to your saddle horn

Longhorn steer, mascot of the city
Beware of Bevo
If you don't say, "hook' em horns"
He won't let you go

Rodeo, Rodeo
Austin Rodeo

It's Austin city here, all is weird
You just let yourself go

Look at this guy, King of Rodeo
He should be damn rich
Ain't it weird to make Rodeo show
Along Congress Avenue bridge

Beautiful sound beautiful voice
For the first time I hear
A singer playing in the front
With a marching band at rear

Rodeo, Rodeo
Austin Rodeo

It's Austin city here, all is weird
You just let yourself go

The sky darkens suddenly, unexpectedly. Travis looks up. Where did that black cloud come from? It takes him a second to realize that he's looking at a storm of bats, the famous Mexican free–tailed bats of Austin. Are they joining the parade too?

Suddenly a million bats
Fly over the parade
I hear they are Mexican
And they are freely tailed

Over the noise, over his own playing, Travis hears a horse scream. It must not like the sight of those bats swirling, darting everywhere. He shakes his head slightly, trying to stay focused. That horse hasn't been properly trained for crowds. Then a woman's shriek follows....

What's happening there, oh my god
Cowgirl's horse got spooked
She's falling off with rope attached
Looks like she's got hooked

Travis stops playing and spins to look. The whole crowd can see what he sees: a golden–haired girl hangs upside–down under the belly of a bolting white filly. He forgets everything else. He doesn't even think about his precious guitar. He just casts it aside and vaults from the float.

> *Music stops, singer boy runs*
> *Gets under the horse,*
> *Catches the rope, calms the horse*
> *Cowgirl safe and sound*

Travis doesn't give a thought to running at the panicked horse. He's glad for all of those years of training. It's still dangerous, but he knows what to do—catch the bridle and calm the animal. He executes each move as if in slow motion. When he can get the filly still enough, he helps the girl get untangled and back on her feet. To the crowd, it looks like something a western Superman would do.

> *The crowds cheer "Travis, Travis"*
> *He's the new hero*
> *His courage made him the star*
> *Of Austin Rodeo*
>
> *Rodeo, Rodeo*
> *Austin Rodeo*

It's Austin city, here all is weird
You just let yourself go

Travis looks at the cowgirl. She's on her feet and she doesn't look hurt, just relieved. When she opens her mouth, he's sure she's going to thank him. Then their eyes meet. Sparks fly. And they both freeze for what seems like forever. Travis finds his voice first:

The boy says "Hi, I'm Travis"
The girl says "Hi, I'm Texy"
Oh my god, that's the start
Of something sexy

Rodeo, Rodeo
Austin Rodeo

It's Austin city here, all is weird
You just let yourself go

Travis stares at the golden–haired girl with the full lips and skin painted lightly with the outdoor Texan sun. She is still gripping his hand tightly. He can feel a colony of butterflies trying to escape his stomach. For a moment the world falls silent, as if there is nothing else in it but her sapphire eyes and her wide smile. But then a rumbling noise begins to creep in.

It's the crowd, which seems to have gone wild. It takes him a moment to realize that they are chanting, "Travis! Travis! Travis!"

Travis? he thinks. That's my name, too!

"I think they're calling you," Texy smiles, "that is, if your name is Travis," finally letting go of his hand.

"I guess I better do what they're asking me to do," he replies.

Travis runs back to his place in the parade, vaults onto the parade float, and picks up his guitar. The crowd cheers again and he feels the energy like electricity running up through the instrument, straight into his heart and out his fingertips and he continues to sing...

Tonight, it's gonna be a long long night, tonight
So light, I feel I'm floating, on a cloud
With my feet, off the ground
Austin, on my mind

My life, I spent my whole life, to be a star
My heart, thanks for keeping up, so far
Endless days, nights too dark
It was hard, how I tried...

I'm flying, "Austin, my dream"

The rest of the parade is a blur to Travis. All he can think about is finding Texy. He can't wait to talk to her again. But a herd of reporters has other ideas. Before he's even off the float, they are swarming around him.

"Travis, how did you know she was in trouble?"

"How does a musician know so much about horses?"

"How did you react so fast?"

"Did you hear her scream over all that noise and music?"

"Travis, how long have you been playing?"

"Travis, look over here and smile for the camera!"

"Travis!"

"Travis!"

"Travis!"

Behind the sea of microphones and cameras, Travis spots his parents, who are waiting to talk to him. His mother is in tears, and he pushes through the reporters to see what the matter is.

She throws her arms around her son. "Oh, Travis, we're so proud! Are you crazy? That horse could have killed you! You sounded great!"

Travis laughs, "Make up your mind, Mom. Are you happy or are you mad at me?"

"Both!" she replies. Next to her, Dad just smiles and slaps his son's shoulder. At least a dozen cameras flash round them. Then Dave emerges from the crowd.

"Well, son, I'm glad I got you a spot on that float!" he says, gripping Travis's hand hard enough to hurt.

"Your dad raised quite the cowboy, and your mom raised a helluva musician."

"I really appreciate the opportunity, sir," Travis insists, "and I'm glad I could make you all proud. That's what I really wanted."

But his eyes are already scanning the crowd, looking for a flash of golden hair. What he really wants right now is another chance to talk to Texy.

[3]

LIVE MUSIC CAPITAL

The Driskill Hotel is humming with excitement as guests arrive for the rodeo gala. A string of limousines snake down Sixth Street bringing Austin's richest and most famous to the event. Upstairs in the historic bedrooms, out–of–town guests are decking themselves in rhinestones and black ties before making their way to the ballroom.

After waving goodbye to his parents, Travis is all gussied up in his finest clothes, and he hopes the girl is bowled over. If he wanted to arrive quietly, though, and continue his mission to find *that* girl, he's going to be very disappointed. The buzz of conversation starts before he's even in the door.

"He's here!" And the cameras are waiting. So are the king of the rodeo and Austin's mayor. They are right by the front door, waiting for him to arrive.

"Here's our hero," shouts the rodeo king, pulling Travis into the lobby. Reporters immediately surround them. "Two great performances in a row—saving that cowgirl and playing awesome tunes! That's quite a debut."

"Thanks," says Travis, a little overwhelmed by it all.

"Tonight you're the guest of honor," the rodeo king goes on into the mic, "and everybody's going to want to shake your hand. But first, we have a question for you."

"This is the live music capital, and since years we've been telling this to the whole world, but it's not enough. We should do some more!." The crowd cheers in response.

"We figure that now it's time to sing it, and we think a guy like you is perfect for that. You're young, you've got talent, courage, and heart—all things that Austin loves! Can you write such a song for Austin? What do you say? Do you want the job?"

Me? Travis thinks. *That's a hard job! Somebody like Willie Nelson or Jimmie Vaughan ought to be doing that!* But the mayor is waiting, the king of the rodeo is smiling, and the crowd is staring. They all want an answer.

"It would be an honor," he finally replies. He finds himself swept into the ballroom on a wave of cheering and the light of sequined gowns.

Someone puts a beer in his hand, but he hardly has time to take a swig because everyone wants to shake the other hand. *When is this going to stop?* he wonders, exasperated. *I'm never going to find her if this keeps up!*

Turns out Travis doesn't need to worry because ten minutes later, the room goes silent and the crowd parts like the Red Sea. There in the doorway stands Texy, glowing in a curve–hugging dress. Next to her stands an elegant blonde—older, but otherwise Texy's twin—in a bright red number so tight that it could make a bull think twice about charging. They spot Travis right away and Texy makes straight for him.

It's hard to say who's grinning wider—the cowgirl or her hero. The lady in red doesn't give either of them a chance to speak. She steps up and grabs Travis by the hand. It's a grip that could crush a walnut. In a Dallas society twang, she calls out, "So you're the young man who saved my baby girl! I've always said, 'Thank God for quick–thinking cowboys! You can't run a successful ranch without them!'"

The crowd laughs and Texy steps in close. "Travis, this is my mama."

He looks down; Mama's still got his hand in a tight grip. "I run the Rancho Austinado, and we help sponsor this rodeo. Texy and the ranch are the *only* things I really love in this life. So I do thank you for what you did today. You'll have to come play your songs for one of our parties sometime."

He's known her thirty seconds, but Travis can see that Texy's mom has a powerful personality. He's just wondering if he'll ever have a moment alone with her daughter. Luckily, the king of the rodeo steps up.

"Those photographers want a picture of the kids, Mama," he chuckles. "You come get some bubbly with me and let's talk some business about this rodeo show."

Mama doesn't look happy to go, but she lets the rodeo king slip her arm through his and flashes him a very impressive white smile before looking back at Texy and Travis.

As they pose for the cameras, Texy whispers to Travis, "Sorry if Mama came on strong. She's very protective. Daddy died when I was two, so I'm all the family she has."

"I can tell. And I can see where you got your looks! She must have been a beauty queen when she was your age."

Texy blushes. "She was! And a model, too. But now she has the ranch to run all by herself, so she wants me to kinda take up that crown."

"Yeah? You gonna be the next Miss Texas?"

"I hate pageants. I really want to be an actress. Give me Hollywood over Dallas any day! I'm lucky, though. Mama thinks I could be a great actress, and she's been doing everything she can to help me live that dream."

"My mama's the same," Travis nods, then chuckles. "Now, my dad on the other hand...."

Eventually, the photographers let Travis and Texy go, scattering to take pictures of the rich and other famous people in the crowd. Finally free, they wander around the room, talking to others at times but with eyes for nothing but each other. She tells him about her favorite movies, the kind of parts she wants to play, and what she'd do if she was famous. He tells her about the songs he's written, the places he wants to play, and the musicians he loves best. They talk about their homes, their parents, and the differences between life in a small town versus that in the big city. They don't notice the fancy food, the expensive champagne, the people ... or Texy's mother, whose eyes are on the couple no matter where they go. Mama watches her precious girl and that country boy like a hawk. If Texy had noticed, she'd have recognized the frown and known what it meant: Mama sees something that makes her real un-happy. And she's gonna do something about it.

But Texy doesn't notice, because her heart is beat-ing twice as fast as usual thanks to this boy whose arm is looped through hers. And boy does he look fine! As they walk and talk, people occasionally stop Travis and Texy—complimenting Travis on his songs, or his work with the filly, or to ask Texy if she's recovered from the shock. But these people don't stay long; they can tell there's no room in this conversation for more than two. Then a round fel-low in a fancy suit and shiny shoes puts himself in their path, and they know that he doesn't plan to move without having a serious talk first.

"Hello, young man! Lovely lady! H.B. Bald." He sticks out a thick hand and gives them each a vigor-ous shake. "I gotta say, Austin is a nice change from L.A."

"Oh," gasps Texy, suddenly all ears. "Are you in film?"

"I am. I produce. Had a little success with a few action films, made a little cash, and now I'm gonna have some fun making more of the kinds of movies I love. Westerns have always been my passion. Travis, that rodeo song was a great one, and I'd love to have it for my upcoming movie. Could I buy you a drink tomorrow and tell you about the soundtrack?"

For a moment, Travis is so stunned and thrilled he can only stare. When Texy elbows him, he finally nods hard enough to snap his own neck.

Texy has a little more poise, and a mama who taught her that a lady always knows how to keep a conversation going, so she asks, "I'd love to know more about the film. What's the plot?"

Mr. H.B. Bald doesn't need coaxing. "We're pretty excited about it. It's all about a cowgirl, her ranch, and her fight to save it from a greedy banker...."

Travis is barely listening, still dazed by the news that Bald wants to buy his song. But a tiny voice in his head reminds him: *Hey, dummy. She just told you she wants to be a movie star. Quick, let this Bald guy know he should give her an audition!* Travis finds his voice.

"You know, Mr. Bald, Texy here is a great actress. She can dance, too. She's taken lessons since she was five. She's got a lot of different talents, and I'll bet she'd be great in your movie.

"Is that so?" says Bald, giving Texy a long once-over with his filmmaker's eye. "Well, Texy, would you like to come out and read for a part?"

"I would love it!" she gasps.

"I'll see what I can do."

"But, oh," says Texy, "you should come out and see the ranch while you're here. My mama runs Rancho Austinado. If westerns are your favorite, you'll love our place. Want to come for lunch tomorrow?"

"Well that's an invitation no man should refuse," interrupts the rodeo king, who has managed to slip up on them all. "H.B., you tell this pretty girl yes, then you come on with me. I want to introduce you to some folks."

"I can't wait to see a real Texas ranch!" he says to Texy before heading off into the crowd with the rodeo king.

Travis and Texy are breathless with excitement—are both of their dreams about to come true? They step out on the balcony, hoping the night air will clear their heads. The sounds of Sixth Street drift up from below.

"I love it here," says Travis, "The lights of all those bars and honky-tonks are like sparks in the dark. I love that we have every kind of music in one place: rock, country, punk, blues, and jazz. We have it all!"

"Well, I think the guest of honor has been at the party long enough," replies Texy, with her eyes full of trouble. "What do you say we sneak on out of this party and go hear some music?"

Travis doesn't need to be asked twice. He grabs her hand and heads straight for the door. They run down the back stairs, giggling like two kids up to no good, and burst out of the hotel doors into the noise and chaos of Sixth Street.

Hand in hand, they join the crowd.

They hear the men on the street singing...

Down on the street,
Don't you hear
Sounds are coming
From everywhere

We're playing to our best,
Our songs are blessed
It's live music in the air

Live music capital,
Center of the world
All is weird here
Sing it Austin

Live music capital
Live music capital
Live music capital of the world

Live music capital
Live music capital
Live music capital of the world

Austin, Austin, Austin, Texas
Austin, Austin, Austin, Texas

Bring your voice and
Bring your ass
Ain't no money
For underwear

Sing rock, country,
Punk, blues, jazz
We feel like
A billionaire

Live music capital
Center of the world
All is weird here
Sing it Austin

Live music capital
Live music capital
Live music capital, of the world

Live music capital
Live music capital
Live music capital of the world

Austin, Austin, Austin, Texas
Austin, Austin, Austin, Texas

Bring your voice and
Bring your ass
Ain't no money
For underwear

Sing rock, country,
Punk, blues, jazz
We feel like
A billionaire

Live music capital, center of the world
All is weird here, sing it Austin

Live music capital
Live music capital

Live music capital, of the world
Live music capital
Live music capital
Live music capital, of the world

Austin, Austin, Austin, Texas
Austin, Austin, Austin, Texas

Live music capital of the world
Live music capital of the world
Live music capital of the world
Live music capital of the world

TEXAS WEATHER
(SHADOW QUEEN)

Travis and Texy would have been happy to spend
all night exploring the musical buffet of Dirty Sixth,
but that doesn't suit Mama. As the rodeo party
winds down, she scans the crowd for her daughter.
That golden hair is nowhere in sight, and that
scruffy musician seems to be missing, too. She sends
a text.

Time to head home.

Then she calls the driver for the car and gets into
the back. When it arrives to where Texy said she was
standing, her daughter is obediently waiting on the
curb with Travis at her side, standing a little too
close to him for Mama's comfort. She can see they
are both reluctant to say goodbye, but she manages
to herd her daughter into the back seat and shut

Travis out of the rest of their evening. He leans forward to wave at Texy through the window, and she stares and waves back until she can't see him anymore.

She sighs happily as she leans back against the seat.

"Nice time, baby?" Mama starts, casual as can be.

"Mm–hm!" gushes Texy. "Travis is just the nicest guy. We've got so much in common—both raised on ranches, grew up riding. We both love music and movies. And we both want to be artists!"

"I'm glad y'all had fun." She lets a moment pass. "Have you thought about entering the Ms. Texas competition yet? We need to get started soon if you're..."

"Oh, Mama! I meant to tell you right off," interrupts her daughter. "We met a Hollywood producer tonight. He's going to let me read for his new film, so I asked him to come to the ranch for lunch tomorrow. You don't mind, do you?"

Mind? Now this is news Mama likes. "I can't wait to meet him. I'll have the cook do something special, and we'll make sure he gets the grand tour."

"I knew you'd be as excited as me! Can Travis come, too?"

"Well, I guess that's the least we can do after he pulled you out from under that horse," Mama says, keeping her tone light. "Y'all looked like you were becoming big friends at the party."

She gives a shy smile and gazes out the window for a minute. "I really like him, Mama. He's sweet and funny and brave. He's really talented, too. You should have seen how many girls wanted to talk to him at that party, but he stuck right by me the whole night!"

"You've always been popular, baby. Any boy could see you're special. But you've always been too smart to let any of them distract you."

Texy knows exactly where she's going with this. "Travis is ... different, Mama. He gets my dreams because he has big dreams, too."

"Well, that's fine, honey. But you just keep focused. Tomorrow could be a big break, and if it is, you won't have time for a boyfriend back home." *Especially not a scruffy kid with no money and no family name I've ever heard,* she thinks.

Texy crosses her arms, though, and gets the same stubborn look she's perfected since she was five. It's the one that says, "I'm not gonna let you tell me *no.*" She looks her mother right in the eye.

"We're having breakfast tomorrow, Mama. It's not a proposal. It's not a national emergency. I like him and he likes me, and we're meeting for break-fast."

Mama sighs, "Alright! Don't get huffy on me. I tell you what. Y'all have a nice breakfast and then you can drop by and see Shadow Queen. You can both get your fortunes told."

"Maaaamaaa."

"It'll be fun. I bet he's never seen a fortuneteller. And maybe she can give you some advice about your audition tomorrow. I'll call later tonight and make the appointment, okay?" *And about that boy. I'll ask her to help me nip this in the bud.*

"Okay, Mama. I'm sure he'll think it's a hoot. We'll drop by before we bring Mr. Bald over for lunch."

⌘

"Tell me again why we're here," says Travis. "This lady is your mama's friend?" He is staring up at a giant neon hand on the front of an old house by the highway.

"No, it's like I said while you were inhaling all those pancakes. She's Shadow Queen, and she's real famous. Everybody in the Hill Country knows about her." She points to a line of waiting people that stretches halfway down the block.

"Well, I never heard of her!"

"That's because you're from a podunk little town. You didn't know what *American Idol* was, either!"

"Aw, c'mon."

Texy crosses her arms, which means trouble. "Mama has come to her for advice about the ranch for years. Mama thinks she's better than a stockbroker and a therapist rolled into one!"

"Your mama, the big-time businesswoman and former beauty queen? She believes in fortunetellers?"

"Don't laugh, Travis. She takes it real serious. C'mon in with me. Even if you don't believe, it's fun!"

"You really want to wait in this line?"

Texy giggles and rolls her eyes. "My mama never waits. C'mon." She takes his hand, and Travis knows he'd happily go with her to a hundred worse places than this. They walk around the side, where a smaller door waits. "This is the entrance for her best clients." She reaches under a white stone, "And the key lives right here." Through the door they go...

...and into the darkest room Travis has ever been in. There's a haze of incense smoke, and it feels like they've gone underground. Strange objects hang in the corners, and he can make out the outlines of mysterious statues. He can hardly see a thing other than a voluptuous woman sitting in a high, golden chair at the far end of the room. She really does look like a magic queen, sitting there in a shiny red dress.

In a voice like thunder, Shadow Queen speaks. "Well, look who's here. Been waiting for you, Texy, and your new friend ... whooo! I can feel the vibrations from here."

Travis doesn't quite know what to say to that, but luckily she doesn't wait for either of them to speak. The woman gestures, "Come on over here and give me your hands."

Together, Travis and Texy cross the room, spellbound by the voice.

"I do feel powerful vibrations. Yep, you both got some serious heat in your blood."

Everything she says is in a powerful voice—like an earthquake is shaking the ground. Then for a long moment she is quiet, gripping their hands in each of hers. Travis wonders if this is what a coyote feels like when its paw is in a trap.

"Oh my god!" She suddenly drops their hands like something hot, then exclaims: "It's the best love ever! Y'all are some lucky kids."

Their hands find each other in the dark, confused and excited, dizzy with incense.

Then she adds:

"You better hang on tight. It's gonna be like Texas weather.

> *Don't you see the crowd, right at my door*
> *It's their destiny they wanna know*
>
> *I'm the fortune teller, the Shadow Queen*
> *You're gonna hear, what you paid for*
>
> *I don't need no crystal ball*
> *Because weather tells me all*

She's got an amazing voice," Travis whispers to Texy. "I've never heard anything so dominant. It's like cannon fire. I should get her to sing the city song."

"Shut up and listen!" Texy shushes him, hypnotized.

> *You come and wonder, how true is your love*
> *Let me tell you, I feel your vibe*
>
> *Your eyes are drowning in the flood of your love*
> *You've got heat in your blood*
>
> *With ups and downs, the best love ever*
> *But it looks like Texas weather*

Texas weather, yeah, Texas weather, yeah

I live in shadow, I live in dark
Rain or sunshine, I never go out

I'm the fortune teller, the Shadow Queen
Don't you mess with Texas weather

Texas weather, yeah, Texas weather, yeah

One day sunshine, the other rain
One day bright, then hurricane

With ups and downs, the best love ever
But it looks like Texas weather

He's mesmerized, but for half a second, Travis wonders *Is a love like a hurricane really a good thing? Sounds a little scary if you think about it.* But the incense and that voice, louder than gale force winds, blow the thought from his mind.

You come and wonder, how true is your love
Let me tell you, I feel your vibe
Your eyes are drowning in the flood of your love,
You've got heat in your blood

With ups and downs, the best love ever
But it looks like Texas weather

Texas weather, yeah, Texas weather, yeah

I live in shadow, I live in the dark,
Rain or sunshine, I never go out

I'm the fortune teller, the Shadow Queen,
Don't you mess with Texas weather

Texas weather, yeah, Texas weather, yeah

One day sunshine, the other rain
One day bright, then hurricane

With ups and downs, the best love ever
But it looks like Texas weather

Texas weather, yeah, Texas weather, yeah
Texas weather, yeah, Texas weather, yeah

Shadow Queen is now deep in a trance, eyes closed, continuously repeating:

Texas weather, yeah, Texas weather, yeah
Texas weather, yeah, Texas weather, yeah

For a moment, they don't know what to do. But Shadow Queen's eyes are tightly closed, as if she has forgotten they are there. She doesn't even notice when the young people leave, slipping out the side door.

The sudden daylight is blinding and their heads are foggy with incense.

Dazed, Travis murmurs, "I never heard a voice like that before. It was like being in a real hurricane!"

Texy pinches his arm. "Is music all you can think about? What about the things she said?"

Travis starts to grin. "Which things was that?"

"You were there, too! You heard her!" Now Texy is grinning back.

And now they are kissing and Texy is whispering, "Didn't you say your hotel was close by?"

[5]

MAGIC IN THE AIR

Travis and Texy's kissing continues in her Jeep hot and heavy, so much so that they have no memory of the drive.

The air in the hotel feels as sexy and hypnotic as it did at Shadow Queen's house, only it's also filled with the thrill of promise. Their noses are still full of the magical scent of the fortuneteller's throne room—an aphrodisiac indeed. They have no eyes for anything but each other, and nothing else in the world to do.

Travis stares into Texy's eyes while he runs his fingers through her hair. Texy sings.

Hold me tight,
Wanna feel your heart
Beating next to mine

Hold me tight
Wanna feel your skin
Melting into mine

There's magic in the air
Run your fingers through my hair

Feel me,
Kiss me
My lips burning with desire
My body trembling, I'm on fire

Feel the magic in the air
Run your fingers through my hair

Hold me tight
Wanna feel your heart
Beating next to mine

Hold me tight
Wanna feel your skin
Melting into mine

Feel the magic in the air
Run your fingers through my hair
Feel me
Kiss me

My lips burning with desire
My body trembling, I'm on fire

Feel the magic in the air
Run your fingers through my hair

Feel the magic in the air
Run your fingers through my hair

Travis thinks he might just lie in one spot all af-
ternoon, staring at Texy's face as she sleeps, the sun-
light from the window lighting up her hair like a
wildfire. Then noise erupts from his cellphone on
the nightstand and she's sitting up, stretching. He de-
cides not to answer, wondering who'd be calling him
right now anyway, but he checks the screen just to
make sure.

"Oh god!" he yelps, "Mr. Bald!"

"What time is it?" she cries, hand over her mouth,
"We were supposed to pick him up at noon!"

Travis fumbles with the phone, "Hey there, Mr.
Bald! ... No, no we didn't forget about you. It's just
traffic in town is really bad with all of the rodeo
stuff ... yeah, almost as bad as L.A.! But we're headed
your way. We should be pulling up in about twenty
minutes.... Yup, see you then!"

There's a hustle and a fuss as clothes and boots are
pulled off the furniture, thrown on, and a mad dash
is made for the car.

⌘

Bald and his director, Tony, are waiting outside the hotel when they arrive, absorbed in their smartphones. They slide into the back of Texy's Jeep and she points it south, heading for the city limits.

They make small talk for a while, and Travis is relieved that Mr. Bald doesn't seem mad about having to wait. Travis does his best to pay attention, though his mind is really on something else—what Texy's mom is going to say. One thing gets through—Mr. Bald mentions that once upon a time, he dreamed of being a famous trumpet player.

"Is that a fact?" Travis looks impressed.

"Oh yeah. I was in a ska band in college and everything. But I got a job as a production assistant right after I graduated and suddenly I had no life outside of film. Sometimes when I am by myself on long flights, I still write down horn arrangements for popular songs on napkins, and I still practice my trumpet when I get a few minutes alone at home."

"Umm yeah!" Travis lies to Mr. Bald.

"Sounds like you've still got the music bug in your blood. Which genre of music are you interested in?" Travis asks.

"Mostly variations of blues from standard to pop, even rock. But I only heard you singing country music, young man. Was this for the rodeo only, or do you sing blues too?

"Umm, yeah!" Travis lies to Mr. Bald.

He starts to realize that the song for Austin should not be a simple country song like the ones he's singing, but a song with a big band to impress the listeners.

He says nothing more, but he wonders if there's an opportunity there. *You never know when a song might sound better with horns,* he thinks. *I wonder if I could twist his arm on this Austin song.*

[6]

RANCHO AUSTINADO

Texy turns off the highway onto a country lane. They stop in front of a massive, fancy gate with "Rancho Austinado" worked in metal across the top. A man with a huge mustache and a huge truck is waiting for them there. Texy slows. "I'm gonna head on up to the house and help Mama finish getting lunch together. Then I'm gonna look at that script you faxed over, Mr. Bald. Roy is going to take you on a tour of the ranch."

The men pile into Roy's truck and Texy's jeep disappears, leaving a dust trail behind.

Fifteen minutes after passing the gate, Roy continues to drive. Travis looks around. He can already tell that this place is way, way bigger than his parents' spread. "Hey Roy, what kind of acreage are we looking at?"

Roy puts the car in park, squints into the sun, and gestures to the horizon on the right. "Everything that way as far as the eye can see is the ranch," he says. He points straight ahead, then behind him, then left. "Everything that way, that way, and that way, too."

They drive past pastures full of cattle and paddocks full of quarter horses. When Mr. Bald asks how many there are, Roy casually mentions, "Oh, 'bout two hundred horses. Last count of the cattle was about thirty thousand head, but we're getting ready to sell off a lot of beef now that we got 'em fattened."

They are some of the finest animals Travis has ever seen, even after years of working the rodeos. He cranes his neck. I think that one's the little filly that nearly broke Texy's neck the other day. Thank you, darlin'! I owe you more than you'll ever know.

"Hey, look H.B.," the director calls, pointing at a row of turning pumps off to the left.

"Oil wells, too?" Bald replies, clearly impressed.

"Yep," Roy replies. "We call that kind a dancing donkey. Texy's grandparents were smart folks. They didn't sell the oil rights when everybody else around here was taking the gas companies' cash. They make a lot more from the leases."

Oil, too? How rich are these people?

A big, beautiful house appears on the right. They can see a swimming pool glittering in the back. To Travis's surprise, they drive right past it. Roy jerks his thumb at it and says, "Guesthouse. The boss likes her friends and relatives to be comfy, but not too close."

"Gorgeous!" says Bald. "That looks better than some of the five-star hotels in L.A."

That's way bigger than our house. That may be bigger than my high school! How big is the place where she actually lives?

They pass a pavilion and picnic ground. "Oh my god!" The director points. "That would be an amazing place to shoot the wedding scene."

"The boss holds a public picnic here every summer. Everybody from three counties shows up. She has a big-name band play and gives the money to charity. Hey, kid. Maybe you'll be the opening act someday." Roy laughs at his own joke.

Travis is not sure if the old guy is trying to yank his chain, but he's not offended. *Hell, I'd do that in a heartbeat.* He can hear Bald and his director talking, hands waving, excited about everything they see, imagining the shot setups and scenes that could play out here.

Now the ranch house itself comes into view, and for a moment everyone in the truck is silent. They stare. *Holy crap.* Travis is thankful everyone is looking ahead and there's no one to see him pick his jaw up off the ground. *That's not a house. That's where Scarlett O'Hara would live.* But there's no time to sit around collecting dust. The front door is opening. It's time to get out of the car, go inside, and face the music.

Texy and Mama are standing on the porch as the men walk up. Travis wants to run straight to Texy, grab her up in his arms, and swing her round and round, but her eyes are saying *wait.* She steps to his side and takes his hand.

They watch Mama turn on her magic and her thousand-watt smile; she knows right away which one is the man who can start her daughter's career. "You must be Mr. Bald. So nice to have you here. You must be *so* busy, so it's awful nice of you to make the time. Did Roy make sure you got to see the ranch on the way in?"

It's the quietest Travis and Texy have ever seen Bald. For half a minute he just stares at Mama. Then he pulls himself together. "This is a great place you've got! My director, Tony, and I were going crazy imagining all the filming you could do in a place like this. Hollywood guys dream about stuff like this!"

Mama takes his arm and leads him inside.

⌘

Inside, Mama moves into the next phase of her charm offensive. Staff members are waiting in the entry hall with cold beers and icy margaritas. There are snacks waiting, and an even bigger spread will be ready for lunch. No one is going to think she's not the most generous hostess in three counties. Not today. Gratified, she can hear Tony and Travis expressing their admiration.

Bald is oddly silent, but Mama's got a lot of experience with men. She notices how he looks into her eyes, how he smiles. Of course, it won't do for him to get too distracted, even if the attention is flattering. That audition has got to happen come hell or high water. But the day is shaping up perfectly so far.

Except for that boy. Why is he still hanging around? Mama doesn't like that at all, but she'll keep quiet for now. Everything else is going just fine.

⌘

The sun is sinking low when the front door opens again.

Now Mr. Bald is emerging from the house, gushing. "A beautiful girl born and raised on a big ranch; who could ask for better when you're looking to cast a cowgirl?" Mama watches Bald and Tony, the director, exchanging excited glances. She knows he won't give any guarantees today, but everything looks very promising indeed. There's every reason to expect good news tomorrow, Mama believes.

He shakes the ladies' hands, saying, "That's a talented girl you've got there! And she's almost as beautiful as her mother."

"You're a flatterer, Mr. Bald," replies Mama, "just the kind of man I like best! Well, that'll be Enrico with the car. I've arranged for him to take all of you gentlemen back to town."

Sure enough, a shiny new sedan is pulling up in the driveway.

"Oh, Mama," objects Texy, "I was going to give them a ride. No need to interrupt Rico's dinner!"

"Nonsense," Mama cuts her off, "Mr. Bald and our director are used to something more comfortable than that Jeep you insist on driving. You need an early night, baby. Catch up on your rest after that big party."

"Thanks again for your hospitality," says Bald, still gripping Mama's hand. "We'll be in touch. I'll let you know what I hear after I talk to the money men back in L.A." At last he lets go, turns, and gets in the car.

Mama knows Travis has no choice but to follow.

⌘

In the car, Bald can hear Tony, the director, talking film with Travis, who wants to know more about the western they're going to film. He can tell what the boy really wants to know is whether Texy's going to get a part. And she probably will. She's a beauty, for sure, and the camera's going to love her. She's a good little actress, too, and will probably be better with some coaching. But somehow he really can't keep his thoughts on Texy. He doesn't have much to add to the conversation, either. His mind is preoccupied with thoughts of someone else....

Long years in film have made him tough and jaded. He's managed to bury his romantic streak beneath layers of cool, hard–assed negotiating, but one look at Texy's mom brought something back to life.

It feels strange. It's more than a little unsettling. But it also feels ... good. *God,* he thinks, *no one would believe it. But it's true. Love at first sight.*

Heading towards San Antone
Driving under beating sun
They say it's the biggest ranch in town

They say there are cows and horses
Cowboys, broncos and longhorns
But damn, I don't remember at all

Rancho Austinado
Rancho Austinado
In my heart
In my soul

Stepped in that big ranch house
Found her standing in front of us
A rancher with beautiful eyes

This beauty made me feel so high
I started to lose my mind
Don't you believe in love at first sight

Rancho Austinado
Rancho Austinado
In my heart
In my soul

Rancho Austinado
Rancho Austinado
In my heart

In my soul

Since then everywhere I go
I keep that feeling
In my heart
In my soul

Rancho Austinado
Rancho Austinado
In my heart
In my soul

Since then everywhere I go
I keep that feeling
In my heart
In my soul

Rancho Austinado
Rancho Austinado
In my heart
In my soul

DANCE WITH ME, MOM

The front door of the ranch house closes and Texy turns to her mama, face lit up with happiness and excitement. "Oh, that was amazing. Today was the best day!"

Mama's grinning just as big. "You got a part, baby; I just know you did. There's no way that man is gonna let you go."

Texy's smile turns devilish, and she waves a finger in her momma's direction. "I don't know.... I think he might cast *you* instead. He couldn't stop looking at you all day."

"Well, I always wanted to see Hollywood. I wouldn't say no...." She walks over to the hall mirror and runs a hand over her stiff hair.

"Mama!" Texy tries her best to look shocked and disapproving, but she can't keep a straight face and they both bust out laughing. Texy's thoughts travel automatically to the boy who's been constantly on her mind.

"Oh, I can't wait to call Travis and tell him about it. Why didn't they let him just stay in the room while I read?"

Mama's laughter stops short and her face that was happy for her daughter a moment before is now stony. "They didn't want you to get distracted. And, honey, neither do I. You listen here. Travis is a nice boy, and he's nice looking, and he did us a big favor saving you from that horse. We'll make sure and send him a thank–you gift. But Texy, this could be the start of a big career. This is the beginning of everything you've ever dreamed you could do. You don't have time for distractions."

Texy sighs. She's so tired of Mama telling her what she should be doing and thinking. "Mama, I'm not getting distracted. And even if I was, Shadow Queen said..."

Mama's face turns a shade of red and Texy can see her fists clench. "I don't care two hoots for what Shadow Queen said! You need to keep your eyes on *your* future!"

For a half second Texy just stands there. Mama has never, not once, questioned Shadow Queen, and they both know it. Then she smiles Mama's favorite smile. "Aw, let's not ruin the mood. It's been a perfect day, and everything's going our way, Mama. C'mon. Dance with me."

> *Dance with me mom, dance with me*
> *I wanna be in your arms again*
> *Dance with me mom, dance with me*
> *Make me feel the same again*
>
> *Come close to me, hold me tight*

I missed you so, here's the hug
This is your song, dance all night
Dance, dance, dance, dance

Dance with me mom, dance with me
I wanna be in your arms again
Dance with me mom dance with me
Make me feel the same again

You're the best mom, excellent cook
Elegant lady, you've got the look
Still charming and cool
Cool, cool, cool, cool

Dance with me mom, dance with me
I wanna be in your arms again
Dance with me mom, dance with me
Make me feel the same again

Being what you want was hard to be
I'm what I'm today, be proud of me
You made it mom, please pray for me
Pray, pray, pray, pray

Dance with me mom, dance with me
I wanna be in your arms again
Dance with me mom, dance with me
Make me feel the same again

I may not be with you, everyday

I may not show my love, every way
Cheer up with this song and pray
Pray, pray, pray, pray

Dance with me mom, dance with me
I wanna be in your arms again
Dance with me mom, dance with me
Make me feel the same again

[8]

AUSTIN HOLDS A PLACE

It's a nervous week for Mama while she waits for Mr. Bald to call. Texy's anxious, too, although she has someone to help her focus on other things.... But they're both beyond ready when Texy's cellphone rings.

"Hello?"

"Texy? Bald here. How's our girl today?"

"Just fine, Mr. Bald. How are you?" Her insides are in knots. She can see Mama across the room, frozen, with a watering can in her hands.

"Well, Texy, we want you to play our cowgirl."

Thrilled, Texy begins to jump up and down, trying to keep it as quiet as she can. She wants to shout out loud, but a lady doesn't bust her producer's eardrums. She can see Mama jumping around across the room, too, hands over her mouth.

Texy gets it together. "I'm just thrilled. Thank you so much."

"Listen. We need you to get out here in L.A. right away. Tomorrow if you can."

"I'll start packing now and be there as soon as I can."

"Great," says Bald. "But tell Mama and Travis they have to stay in Austin for now. We're going to need you in meetings and fittings all day every day. You have to be completely focused on your work."

"Oh, they'll be so disappointed!"

"Being a star is going to mean sacrifice. And Texy, if you want it, you can be a big, big star."

Texy hangs up.

"You got the part! I'm so proud of you. Honey, that's amazing! So why do you look like Rover just died all over again?"

"Mr. Bald says I have to come out as soon as I can. And I have to be by myself. I can't bring you and I can't bring Travis."

Mama's quiet for a minute. "You need to do what he says for now. I'll come to Hollywood in a few days; I won't leave my baby all alone in a strange place. I'm sure they'll let me visit the set soon. I'll even get an apartment in L.A. so we can be together whenever you have time."

"Mama, how can you leave the ranch? You've never lived anywhere but Texas. And who's going to manage everything here while you're gone? This place needs you!"

Mama's not listening. She's walking across the room, calling, "Get Texy's bags packed; she's going to Hollywood. And start packing up my stuff, too!"

Mama's just left the room when Travis walks in. "Hey, gorgeous," he says, kissing her cheek, "You should see the gift your Mama sent me—that guitar must have cost her a bunch. I thought she didn't like me much, but she sent me a nice note about getting you off that horse. Have a look."

Travis holds out the card, but she doesn't take it. All he gets in return is a weak little grin. "What's wrong?"

"I got the part."

Travis whoops. "That's amazing! I knew you would. That's just ... that's ... so why aren't you turning cartwheels around this room?"

"Bald says I have to come alone. He says I won't have time for you or Mama."

"Huh? What's she say about that?"

"Oh, she's planning to fly out a few days after me. She's not going to let Bald or anyone else tell her what to do. But Travis, I don't know what the ranch will do without her here. *She* is the family business. She shouldn't be leaving it behind ... and I don't know when I'm going to see you again...."

Travis sticks Mama's note back in his pocket and sits next to Texy, taking her hand. "Hey," he says softly, "it's gonna be okay. You know, in my childhood, when things were not going well, my mom would sing to me. 'Austin Holds a Place for Those Who Pray.' C'mon, now. We can sing it together."

They hold each other's hands and start.

> *When you feel all alone*
> *When you are down and out*
> *When suddenly you start crying*
> *Like you've never done before*
>
> *Oh darling just take me in your arms*
>
> *When you feel left behind*
> *When you feel like giving up*
> *When suddenly you're feeling*
> *Like you've never done before*
>
> *Oh darling just take me in your arms*
>
> *Hold my hand and let me show you the way*
> *Austin holds a place for those who pray*

Just take me in your arms
That's all I ask from you

Hold my hand and let me show you the way
Austin holds a place for those who pray
Just take me in your arms
That's all I ask from you

When your heart is full of love
When your mind is full of hope
When suddenly you cheer up
Like you've never done before

Oh darling please take me in your arms

Hold my hand and let me show you the way
Austin holds a place for those who pray
Just take me in your arms
That's all I ask from you

Hold my hand and let me show you the way
Austin holds a place for those who pray
Just take me in your arms
That's all I ask from you

AUSTIN SAVE MY LOVE

If Travis thought his words might make Texy feel a little better, he's managed to achieve the exact opposite. She was crying before; now she's sobbing loud enough to be heard all over the house.

"I don't know what to do, Travis," she wails. "I want to be a movie star so bad. But I don't know if I can leave home. I don't want Mama to have to leave the ranch. And I sure don't think I can stand not to see you for God knows how long."

She takes a deep breath and Travis hopes she might be calming down. Nope. "I'm not going. That's it. I'm just not going to go." With that, she runs from the room.

Thirty seconds later, before Travis has had time to decide what to do next, Mama comes running in. "What on earth happened? Did you say something to my baby?"

"No! I was just trying to help!"

"Well she's gone and locked herself in her room. She won't come out and she won't say anything except 'I'm not going.' What does that mean?"

"She's upset about leaving home. She's afraid of what will happen to the ranch if you both move to L.A. And she is sad about not seeing m—us for a long time."

Mama gives him a long look and Travis thinks the temperature in the room might just go subarctic. Finally, she says quietly, "I think you ought to go on home, Travis. Y'all have had a lot of fun, but she doesn't need to get too serious too fast. It'll just confuse her more. I think she'll be better off if you give her a little space."

"You're the one who oughta give her some space. She wouldn't be having second thoughts if you weren't threatening to leave the ranch and hover over her in Hollywood."

"Go home, Travis. Just get in that beat–up old truck and go."

Travis doesn't have much of a choice. Mama has several tough men working the property, and he knows she won't hesitate to have them "escort" him off her land. He turns and walks out of the house.

Heading out to his truck, Travis clenches his fists.
What do I do? he wonders, desperately. I don't want
to lose her. *I don't want her to lose her big chance.*
He feels full of dynamite, ready to explode. *I don't
know what I can do. I can't make Mama stay home. I
don't know if they'd let me see her out there. I don't
know how I could live without her. Who can help
me?*

He sings:

You say you changed all your plans
And wanna move to golden lands
I find no words to say

In my tangled state of mind
Trying hard to keep that brain of mine
Don't you know, you're fooling me, oh yeah

I don't wanna think about it
I don't want, losing you

I don't wanna think about it
I don't want, losing you

Fame and glory sealed your eyes
I should find a compromise
Austin save my love

People around you will make me fight
I feel like a dynamite
I'm gonna find a way, tonight

I don't wanna lose control
I don't want, losing you

I don't wanna lose control
I don't want, losing you

People around you will make me fight
I feel like a dynamite
I'm gonna find a way, tonight

In my tangled state of mind
Trying hard to keep that brain of mine
Don't you know, you're fooling me, oh yeah

I don't wanna think about it
I don't want, losing you

Losing you
Losing you

Austin save my love
Austin save my love

Austin save my love
Austin save my love

Travis is in his truck, his hands holding the wheel in a death grip, and suddenly, a bolt of lightning strikes the road ahead. The sound of a sudden, heavy rain fills his ears. He sighs, "Typical Texas weather."

And then a voice echoes in his head,

"With ups and downs, the best love ever,
But it's like Texas weather …
One day sunshine, the other rain,
One day bright, then hurricane."

"You were right," he says, "We were so good together. We were up and everything was great. Now we're down.... Does this mean that we'll be up again? Can Shadow Queen actually see the future?"

Travis finally gets why Texy's Mama believes what Shadow Queen tells her. She's been right about everything so far. But what's going to happen next? Do Shadow Queen's words mean that their love will be "up" again? If that's the case, then he can make some new plans. He breathes a quick prayer to the city: "Thank you, Austin, for reminding me of Shadow Queen." Now he needs to talk to her again. Face to face. As soon as possible.

Travis sticks the key in the ignition, guns the motor, and hits the gas. No time to waste.

⌘

The lightning strikes 'til he makes it to Shadow Queen's house in the evening.

It seems like half of Austin has the same idea. Even though it's pouring down rain, there's still a crowd of waiting customers. Luckily, Texy showed him what to do. He slips around the side and finds the key under the white stone. He lets himself in the side door.

It's even darker than it was last time. Before Travis's eyes have time to adjust, he hears her voice.

"Weather told me someone was comin' … I was waiting for someone. I just didn't know who it would be. Come close and let me see you."

There she is on her throne. She gives a deep, throaty laugh. "Hey, lover boy. So you're the one the weather sent me? Must be important if you're here at this hour of the night. And sneaking in the side door, too. So, why don't you tell me about it?"

Travis is suddenly nervous. He's still desperate. But he doesn't know exactly what to say.

"Uh. Um." He feels like his boots are nailed to the floor.

"Go on," she says. "I don't want to keep my paying customers waiting too long."

Suddenly, Travis is scared and edgy. He doesn't know how to say what he's come to say. So he stalls. "You got a very powerful voice," he blurts out. "Great voice. Um. You know I've been writing this song ... um ... the city hired me. Uh, I'm supposed to write a song for Austin...." Travis is panicking now, knowing he is babbling like an idiot. He blurts out, "I think Austin deserves to listen to your voice."

Shadow Queen smirks. She can tell he's BS–ing. But she looks a little flattered all the same. "Really? Do I sound that good? Austin deserves my voice? Ha ha ha. Okay, boy, what's the name of your song?"

Travis has no idea. Over the last couple of weeks, he has thought of nothing but Texy. He's not even started on writing that song. "Austin," he stutters.

"Oh, that's a real original title," she laughs.

His heart is sinking, knowing that he's making a complete fool of himself, but then his mother's voice rises from Travis's paralyzed brain, "Austin's where I long to be." And the song starts to write itself.

"Austin, That's Where I Long to Be."

Now Shadow Queen nods, "Not bad. I know the feeling myself. When I was a girl in Waco, I couldn't wait to get here."

Inspiration now firing up his mind, Travis actually forgets for a second why he's come. All he wants is to find a pen and his guitar.

"But now, get to the point, boy," she barks. "Austin deserves my voice, huh? Well that's nice. But it's not why you're really here, now, is it?"

This seems to be the kick in the pants Travis needs. "Well," he says, "it's about the ups and downs of our love. Remember how you said..."

"I remember. Texy's mama called to talk to me about that, too." She chuckles.

"Too many things happened in a very short time. We were really happy and suddenly things started to change. Texy's locked in her room and won't come out. Either she loses me or she loses her chance to be a star. Do you think things will ever be up again? Are you sure?"

Apparently, this was the wrong thing to say. The thunder roars and the fortuneteller rises from her chair, fury in her face. "When I say something, I mean it!"

Travis asks, "Then what can I do? How can I save my love?"

Over the roar of the storm, he hears her dark, ominous voice. "Do whatever you want, but do it now; the weather tells me it's right—the time—so go quick and do it."

Travis is out the side door before she has a chance to say anything else. He feels power in his veins now, sure he can fix this. Austin heard his prayer and is going to help.

How much cash have I got? He sticks a hand in his hip pocket, reaching for his wallet, and comes up with the thank–you card signed by Texy's mom. All of a sudden, he gets a great idea.

Travis goes to an ATM and withdraws all of the cash he has in the world and heads back to his hotel. Most of the airlines are fully booked, but he finds a redeye out to L.A. He'll have to hurry to get everything ready and printed before he gets on that flight.

⌘

On the flight, Travis takes advantage of the quiet and his newfound inspiration to work on the song.

As soon as he hits Hollywood the next morning, he heads straight for Mr. Bald's office. He's got a license agreement for the rodeo song in one hand and a large manila envelope in the other.

"I've brought a signed contract for Mr. Bald," he tells the secretary. "It's the rights to a song."

"You can leave it here," she says, reaching out.

"No, ma'am," he replies quickly. "Sorry, but I was told he had to sign for it personally. Could you just tell him Travis from Austin has arrived?"

She sighs but makes the call. Then, looking surprised, she waves him through to the back office.

Bald looks up from his desk. "Hey there, hero. You came all this way to bring me an agreement? And you left that pretty girl alone on her last day in Austin? How's her mama?"

"Mama's fine." Travis says. For a half second he feels guilty for what he's about to do. Then he thinks *For Texy* and he goes on. "Actually, Mama's been kinda down since y'all left the ranch."

Now he has Bald's full attention. "Oh? She coming down with the flu?"

"No, sir, nothing like that. She just seems a little ... mopey. Like she was missing somebody. Anyway, while I'm here, I want to show you this new song that I'm writing for Austin. I'd like your input on the horn parts." He hands Bald the paper with the song.

"Sure, sure. It would be fun to dust off those old musical chops. Now, you said she's missing someone?"

"Seems like it. Anyway, I want this song to have a really rich, powerful sound. I can't ask anyone in Austin because I don't want them to think I can't handle the responsibility. I don't know anything about arranging horns, and I immediately thought of you. Can you help me with that?"

Bald laughs, delighted. "You know, everyone in the film business has been asking for my help for years. But I think this is the first time I've been asked about my musical ability." He takes a quick look at the paper. "Yeah, I can already hear something for this break—something like *na nan na nanah.*"

"That's great!" Travis nods. He can tell Bald is flattered, but that this isn't really the topic he wants to hear about. At least the trap is set.

Now, Bald walks into it. "I'd love to help you out with this song, Travis. But maybe you could do something for me in return."

"Sure!"

"Tell me more about Texy's mom. Who do you think she's missing? Is there some Austin billionaire in her life?"

Now Travis holds out the envelope and grins. "I'm guessing it's not. Have a look at this."

Mr. Bald pulls out a sheaf of printed papers and looks at them. "What? Is this possible?" he asks, astonished. "Look at this. It says she's offering to let us film at her ranch!"

"I believe so," Travis nods, looking carefully out the window.

"And she's offering to let the cast and crew stay at the guesthouse. And she's going to pay for catering for everyone while we shoot. That's ... very generous. Why would she do this?"

"Well, I think she wrote something in there about 'A real western can only be filmed in an authentic, natural environment.'"

"That's an awfully generous thing to do for authenticity," Bald replies, skeptical.

"If I had to guess," Travis replies, "I'd say she wants to spend some more time with you."

Bald can't help himself. He's grinning like a madman. "You think so?"

"Hey," shrugs Travis, "she signed it, not me."

Bald holds out his hand for Travis to shake. "Well, I guess we'll see you in a few days then. Tell Mama and Texy thank you from the whole company."

"You bet," Travis replies, ready to get out while the getting's good.

"And tell Mama I can't wait to see her!" Bald is already picking up the phone and writing furiously.

Travis lets himself out quietly. Okay, Shadow Queen. Okay, Austin, he prays. This way everybody gets what they want. Texy gets her career and her home. Mama gets to stay close to Texy. And I get to be with the woman I love. I've started writing your song. I have given it my best shot. The rest is up to you.

[10]

AMOR AMOR AMOR

At Rancho Austinado, Mama's cellphone rings. It's a California number, and she braces herself to deal with this call. How is she going to tell them Texy's having second thoughts?

"Hello?"

"Hey there, Mama. Bald here! Let me tell you, you are not just gorgeous, you are one generous lady."

"Thanks?"

"We're still in shock out here. But we're incredibly cited to be joining you at Rancho Austinado. I thought you were just kidding when you said you wanted to break into the movie biz. But you're doing it in a big way, letting us use the whole ranch to film."

Mama is silent for what must be a full minute. Bald finally says, "Hello?"

"Oh, sorry. Just a little distraction in the other room. Texy's, um, calling me. But please, go on."

"Are you sure there's room for everybody at the guesthouse?"

"How many of you ... will there be?"

"Well, with the cast, director, and other key crew, probably thirty. There will be a lot of other folks, too, but we'll rent some campers for them. The actors don't like to sleep too close to the grips and sound guys, you know."

"Of course not," Mama agrees. "And when will you be arriving?"

"A–S–A–P, sweetheart, A–S–A–P. But we'll give you enough time to arrange catering. I know feeding so many people every day for a few weeks takes some serious planning."

"It sure does!" She gasps. She wants to say *What the hell are we talking about? Who invited you here?* It's on the tip of her tongue. But then she realizes: *Having them here will solve all of our problems.*

Maybe Texy has made this offer to Bald. Maybe not. She's still pretty confused, but she's willing to take the rope life seems to be throwing her.

"Well, I've got to get busy planning for y'all to arrive. Filming here is going to make Texy the happiest girl in Texas."

"And I'll be the happiest producer."

"Can't wait to see y'all!" She is eager to hang up the phone and talk to her daughter.

"You too, sweetheart! Thanks again!"

As she ends the call, Roy walks in, hat in hand.

"Hey boss. Just here to pick up the boys' paychecks."

"They're on the desk. Hey, Roy, did Texy say anything to you about bringing that producer and his team back to the ranch?"

"No, ma'am. 'Course I ain't seen her much these days. She spends all her time with that young musician."

"Yeah, I noticed. Well, they're going to be doing some filming here on the property. You'll have to coordinate. Tell them to start getting the guesthouse ready. I'm going to work on catering."

"How long are they staying?"

"A few weeks, they said."

"Lordy, that's gonna cost a fortune, feeding a whole film crew day and night."

"Don't I know it. Well, anything for my baby, right Roy? We better get started."

Roy heads back out to the office and Mama goes to have a chat with her daughter.

⌘

Travis is barely off the plane when his phone rings. It's Texy. He crosses his fingers and says, "Hello."

"Oh my god, Travis, you'll never guess what. It's got to be a miracle."

"You're the miracle, honey. But tell me. What's up?"

"Bald called Mama. They're coming to the ranch to film. I don't have to leave; Mama can keep running the ranch, and I'll be where I can see the guy I like...."

"Texy, that's the best news ever. I told you it would all work out."

"You were right. It was kinda weird, though. Mama seemed to think I might know something about it. But it was a complete surprise."

"Uh huh," Travis replies. The less he says right now, the better.

"Anyway," Texy says breezily, "the whole cast and crew are staying with us. Mama's pretty excited about meeting George, Brad, and the other actors, and she's arranging a huge Tex–Mex fiesta for the night they arrive. I'm inviting you, too."

"I can't wait!" Travis replies.

⌘

The stars are out, the crowd is laughing, and Mr. Bald has jumped on stage with a trumpet to join in on the music. It's the night of the fiesta and Mama has spared no expense. She has brought in San Antonio's best mariachi band; the margaritas are flowing; and the spread of barbecue, enchiladas, tacos, and tamales seems to stretch about a mile.

Amor amor amor   *amor amor amor*
Amor amor amor   *amor amor amor*
Amor amor amor   *amor amor amor*
Amor amor amor   *amor amor amor*

Fiesta,
Tequila,
Margarita,
Cerveza

Amor amor amor   *amor amor amor*
Amor amor amor   *amor amor amor*

Fiesta,
Tequila,
Margarita,
Cerveza

> *Amor amor amor   amor amor amor*
> *Amor amor amor   amor amor amor*

The cast and crew are having a great time, and Texy looks radiant in the new designer denim dress Mama ordered.

Travis is never two steps from her daughter's side. Mama watches him with growing irritation and suspicion. Something about that boy's not right. It's like he's ... guilty about something. Mama can see it in his eyes. She just can't quite put her finger on what he could have done.

But she doesn't have time to investigate, because once he gets off stage, Bald follows Mama everywhere. They dance, they make small talk, and his flirting seems to get a little more obvious every half an hour. She doesn't mind, but he only has half her attention until he says, "I sure was surprised when our young hero turned up in my office."

"Oh?" says Mama, suddenly laser focused and staring at him like a rattler stares at a rabbit.

"Yep. You could have knocked me over with a feather when he said you'd sent him to deliver that contract. But I'm glad you did. I'm glad you wanted to see me—us—again."

Mama nods slowly, "Sure. I'm just thrilled you're here. But tell me, did you bring that contract? I forgot to keep a copy for my records."

"Gave it to that cowboy Roy. I thought your manager might need to have it handy."

"That was smart thinking. Listen, I have to handle some last–minute things for tomorrow, but I'd love to dance again a little later." She gives his arm a friendly squeeze and walks away to find Roy. Eventually she finds him watching the band, longneck in hand.

"Go to the office right now and get me Bald's contract. Come straight back."

"You bet," he says, surprised. "Back here in ten minutes?"

"No, I'm going to go find the sheriff. He was hanging out by the taco bar last time I saw. We'll meet you out on the front porch."

Ten minutes later, she's flipping through the contract on the porch, Roy and the sheriff at her side. "I never wrote this. And I certainly never signed it."

Roy whistles. "Sure looks like your signature, boss. I see yours all the time; this one even had me fooled."

"Well, Travis has got to be the one responsible. H.B. told me he hand–delivered it in L.A."

"Now, where would a cowboy like him learn to forge stuff?" Roy wonders.

Mama might not be surprised to learn that Travis got his start with his own father's signature. Then again, she might not care. "It doesn't matter. He's got to know it's a crime," she snaps.

"What do you want to do about it?" the sheriff asks. "Want me to take him in tonight?"

"No," Mama says quickly. "Let's not ruin Texy's party. Roy, we'll let them stay and film just like it says here in the contract. It's best for Texy. But tomorrow morning, sheriff, you can take that boy straight to jail. I'm pressing charges."

[1 1]

AUSTIN PRISON BLUES

"This is Ed Head with Channel 10 News. In a surprise turn of events, the city's favorite hero Travis has been arrested for forgery."

"Hey, hey. This is Ray Ray with *KSGR*. Big news this morning. Travis is in the pokey. That's right, our hero musician is in trouble with Johnny Law. Turns out his talents also include faking his girlfriend's mother's signature."

"Celia Delia on the scene at the Travis County jail, where a young musician is about to sit behind bars. Just a few weeks ago, he made headlines by saving a local cowgirl from a panicked horse...."

The news media is having a field day with the arrest. Luckily for Mama, the film crew is so busy they don't have time for the news, so Bald and Texy haven't yet found out. Unfortunately for Mama, the sheriff's deputy has a friend who works in the news, so the camera crews are waiting when the patrol car arrives with Travis in the back.

She watches with approval at the TV screen as he stands on the steps of the jail in handcuffs. Her sense of satisfaction quickly fades, however, as he smiles and looks right into the camera. "Yes, I did sign it. But I did it for love!" *What? Does the idiot think that's going to help?*

But the reporters go wild. They are firing a million questions at him, but he looks handsome, charming, even defiant, as he keeps repeating, "I did it for love! Don't take it for a crime!" He stands tall before the cameras, not one inch of shame anywhere on his body.

"You could be going away for a long time," one reporter says.

"I don't think I'll be in there long. The people of Austin won't let me down." Mama can feel her anger bubbling up inside her chest, like a bottle of champagne ready to pop.

"Austin's not big on crime," says another.

"But Austin is big on lovers. Everyone will understand I just wanted to keep Texy from having her heart broken." *The fool thinks he's in love after just a few days.*

"Do you have a message for the people of Austin?"

"I know you won't let me down. You won't leave me behind bars. I'm counting on you, Austin!"

When they finally take him inside, Mama's jaw is on the floor. *That did not go down the way I'd planned.*

⌘

Now in his cell, Travis sits and waits. He feels sure he won't be here long, and he knows what to do next. Now that he's got the time and a quiet space, he can complete his official song for Austin. It's good that he could give the main tune of the song to Shadow Queen at the night of thunder, now he has to write only the lyrics. For horns arrangements, he's luckily got them from Mr. Bald at the fiesta at Rancho Austinado, who prepared them diligently and explained him what to do. Now he will only complete the puzzle in his head. Apparently, he feels very happy to be in jail:

> *First time in my life,*
> *I feel so secure and safe*
> *I slept like a baby,*
> *Such a warm and cozy space*
>
> *Angel cops of Austin*
> *Thanks for serving*

Breakfast lunch and dinner
And the free ride from my home

It was so good to see you
Enjoying your job, guys
But I've got serious doubts
For missing you all

Thank you guys,
I believe it's time to go
I appreciate the service,
But you can't keep me here for long

This is Austin Texas,
I can hear the crowds, they're weird
But won't let lovers
Stay behind bars

One day
When you'll do crazy things for your love
Tell everybody when a lover does,
Don't take it for a crime

Lovers get crazy,
Don't take it for a crime

Lovers get mad, mad, mad, mad
Don't take it for a crime

One day
When you'll do crazy things for your love
Tell everybody when a lover does
Don't take it for a crime

Don't take it for a crime

Don't take it for a crime

Don't take it for a crime

Don't take it for a crime

[12]

AUSTIN MARCHING

The news story gathers momentum. Fast. All day long, Travis's face is on TV, his voice is on the radio, his picture is on social media. Everything shows him saying proudly, "Here in Austin, if you do crazy things for love, people understand. They don't take it for a crime."

And the people of Austin hear Travis. They might not approve of forgery, but they find his naiveté charming. They already know he's brave. And handsome. And talented. It's not hard to want to take his side. And they do.

Protests happen all over town. Crowds gather, carrying signs:

Love Is No Crime in Austin!

HE DID IT FOR LOVE

Set LOVERS free

It soon becomes clear that different groups are converging and heading for the same place—the State Capitol building. A mass of bodies and hair-styles and colorful clothing is moving as one, shouting, demanding its way. The TV trucks are speeding to line up along the protest route. The reporters push to get into the best spots to see the action.

> "This is Celia Delia. Behind me, you can see a huge crowd coming up the street. The woman leading them, in the shiny red dress, is famous local fortuneteller Shadow Queen."

> "This is amazing, music fans. The whole rodeo community has rallied and is riding up Congress Avenue. This is Ray Ray, and I'll keep you tuned into the action as the situation builds."

> "This is Ed Head, and I can't believe what I'm seeing! Oh my God, is that the UT marching band? And is that Bevo they have with them? I believe it is!"

The crowds are chanting, pleading for mercy and Travis's release. They begin to move in time with the marching band.

> *March for love*
> *March for love*
> *March for love*
> *March for love*

Austin city
March for love
Austin city
March for love

Set the lovers free
Set the lovers free

March for love
March for love
March for love
March for love

Austin city
March for love
Austin city
March for love

Set the lovers free
Set the lovers free

[13]

AUSTIN
WHERE I LONG TO BE

The crowds are gathered at the Capitol, shouting, waving signs.

Mr. Bald and Texy are in the Jeep, speeding down the highway. They've dragged Mama along. Texy is hopping mad. She has her back to the car door and her hands are all over the place.

"I cannot believe you did this, Mama! I let you meddle. I let you hover. But this is too much!"

"He's a criminal, baby. He forged my signature. Love has blinded you. It's up to me to save you!" Mama tries to pat Texy's arm, but she pushes her away angrily.

"Travis saved me, Mama. He brought Mr. Bald here."

"He saved me, too," says Bald, looking into Mama's eyes. "I'd never have met you without him."

Mama sighs. "He just can't get away with stealing from us."

"Uggghhh!" shouts Texy. "You're happy to host the film. You didn't cancel when you figured it out. So he's not really stealing, is he?"

Mr. Bald takes Mama's hand. "Just ask yourself. Isn't everybody happier now?"

She can't say no. She sighs again. "Give me the phone. I'll call the sheriff." She spends some time talking while Texy listens to make sure Travis will be back with her soon. "Yes, Sheriff, I withdraw all the charges. Yes, I'm sure." She sighs as she ends the call. The last thing she wants right now is to look like the evil mother in the eyes of the press. It wouldn't be good for business.

Checking his phone, Mr. Bald is beside himself with delight. The best kind of marketing comes in the form of free, viral videos, and he's been given enough material to make a fortune with this movie. He keeps scrolling through his feed. Travis has given them plenty to run with. That boy is a goldmine.

The traffic was built up along IH35 for miles, but when they finally arrive at the Capitol, even Mama can't believe the size of the crowds. "All of these people are here for *that* boy?"

"They sure are!" Texy shouts, joyfully. And then she spots him. Released from jail, the cops have brought Travis to the Capitol steps. Somebody's got to calm this crowd, and police are standing on the edges waiting for orders. Texy runs forward, pushing people out of the way. When they realize who's trying to get through, the crowd parts. People shout, "It's Texy!" and "Let her through!"

She reaches Travis. He throws his arms around her and doesn't want to let her go. They're in the middle of a long kiss when someone nudges him. It's Shadow Queen. "Okay, lover boy. There's time for that later." She hands him a guitar. "Right now it's time to sing your song."

She walks with him up the steps and the crowd goes silent. Travis raises his guitar, grins, and shouts, "Austin, that's where I long to be!"

Shadow Queen starts to sing, then everybody joins.

> *Are you ready for party time*
> *Austin Texas here we come*

Kick off your shoes throw them in the lake
We're gonna dance and booty shake

Hit the road shows and honkey-tonks
Red River and dirty Sixth
Let live music fill your veins

Meet the future Stevie
The braids of old Willie
No limits in this city

Austin, that's where I long to be
Austin, that's where I long to be

Bring your dream and fantasy
Let's all live in ecstasy
So inspired and so indie
We pipe the peace and keep our minds free

Your shorts and sandals good with us
But if you wanna bare it all
You're welcome at Hippie Hollow

If so much love makes you starving
Go to food trucks in the evening
Make friends while you eat

Austin, that's where I long to be
Austin, that's where I long to be

Bring your dream and fantasy
Let's all live in ecstasy
So inspired and so indie
We pipe the peace and keep our minds free

Your shorts and sandals good with us
But if you wanna bare it all
You're welcome at Hippie Hollow

If so much love makes you starving
Go to food trucks in the evening
Make friends while you eat

Austin, that's where I long to be

Austin, that's where I long to be

Austin, that's where I long to be

Austin, that's where I long to be

The crowd starts to sing along once they get the hang of the tune, which is very catchy. Shadow Queen is singing for all she's worth. Travis keeps strumming but slips quietly off the steps with Texy to follow the dancing crowd. They all move down the street like a long colorful dragon. Texy nudges Travis and points. Up ahead he can see Mama dancing with Mr. Bald, who grabs her by the waist and gives her a kiss. She puts her arms around the producer. Texy smiles and says, "Just like Texas weather."

Someone taps Travis's shoulder. It's his mother's old friend Ed, the professor. "This is a great composition, Travis."

"Thanks, Professor. I bet my mom would be glad to know you like it."

He strokes his gray goatee. "You know, you ought to try applying to UT next year. I think our department would be glad to have you."

Travis reaches out to shake the professor's hand. "I'd be proud to!"

Now there's another shout—somehow, amid all the noise and crowds of people, Travis's parents have found them. He can see from their faces that they can't decide whether to kiss him or kick him in the butt. He knows they're going to have something to say about his arrest, even if he did get off. But for now, Mom and Dad push their way up to Travis and throw their arms around their son. They pull Texy into the hug as well.

And in the distance, they all hear the sounds of the LIVE MUSIC CAPITAL.

Down on the street, don't you hear

Sounds are coming from everywhere
We're playing to our best, our songs are blessed
It's live music in the air

Live music capital, center of the world
All is weird here, sing it Austin

Live music capital
Live music capital
Live music capital, of the world

Austin, Austin, Austin, Texas

ABOUT THE AUTHOR

Fehmi Nuhoglu, aka Franky, has been a member and song-writer of several rock bands, composed many songs, and performed in Europe with many local artists.

As a college sophomore in engineering school, he had to put his musical career aside, but Franky remained a private composer/songwriter until he arrived in Austin, TX, in 2008—when his wife, Irem, a UT professor, made her home there.

Affected by the city's unique lifestyle and finding new peace of mind in Austin, Franky returned to songwriting and music composition—which he now balances with his work in engineering.

FIRST SONG FOR AUSTIN, TX:
"Austin, Where I Long to Be"

The project started in 2010, when Franky wrote a rock song about Austin, TX: "Austin, Where I Long to Be." He considers this song a thank–you to the city for the inspiration it has given him since 2008.

When arranging this special song, he wanted a richer sound with a full band, so he rearranged the style of the song to blues–rock–pop so that everyone could sing along.

THE NOVELLA:
A Love Like Texas Weather

As new ideas continued to come to mind, Franky decided to make a whole album about Austin. He wrote a story through which he could describe the city in a better way, creating characters like Travis and Texy and using the tale of their love to promote the city.

THE CONCEPT ALBUM:
Austin, Texas the Rock Opera

Driven by the desire to keep the songs as they were originally written, and to include a diversity of styles including: rock, blues, blues rock, country, R & B, Latino, pop, etc., Franky decided to frame the "concept album" as "Austin Texas the Rock Opera."

THE MUSICAL PLAY:

Although the resulting album is a rock opera, the authentic story and diverse music have driven Franky to write a musical play version, too. At the date of this book's publication, he is still working on it.

AUSTIN TEXAS THE ROCK OPERA:
Making It Happen

Franky wanted to record each song in the birthplace of its genre. He started with blues, turning to the multi–Grammy nominated Joyride Studio in Chicago, IL. Recordings began in January 2016 with Grammy–winning engineer Blaise Barton and Brian Leach. As the project's scope grew, Gravity Studios of IL was also brought on board. Recording and mixing lasted almost six months, ending in July 2016.

Franky travelled all over the country seeking versatile musicians for his band. The first members were Ric Jaz (Rock 'n' Roll Hall of Fame inductee and guitar player for legendary Buddy Guy as well) and Kenny Anderson (Blues Hall of Fame–er and trumpet player for Bill McFarland Chicago Horns Band). Rock 'n' Roll Hall of Fame–ers David Service (bass), Roosevelt Purifoy (keyboards) and Malcom L. Banks Sr (drums) soon joined, as well. At the end of several auditions, Franky decided on Jennifer Williams as female vocalist and Brian Leach as singer, multi–instrumentalist and engineer.

World–class music professionals supported the band, and many songs feature guest artists like Lynne Jordan, Theo Huff, the Hoyle Brothers, John Rice, Matthew Skoller and Bill McFarland Chicago Horns, to name a few.

All 13 songs of the concept album are composed, arranged, lyrics written, co–mixed, produced, and copyrighted by Franky. Five horn arrangements and two string arrangements were made by Kenny Anderson, meanwhile one horn arrangement is made mutually by Franky and Kenny Anderson.

The process has taken hundreds of hours of rehearsing and studio time so far. Franky has spent several weeks in studios, assisting to the whole rehearsing, recording, and mixing sessions.

The mixes were mastered by Jerry Tubb in Terra Nova, the multi–Grammy nominated studio in Austin, TX.

Meanwhile, two editors worked on the novella written by Franky to accompany the album. And Dick Reeves, the 2016 Grammy winner from Austin, TX, was commissioned to design artwork for the whole project, including the CD album cover and the novella cover.

ACKNOWLEDGMENTS

This album and book project is a tribute to Austin, TX, which deeply inspired me with its diversity in music, unique lifestyle, and tranquility.

To all of the most incredible musicians, soulful singers, engineers, artists, and everyone involved with Franky and the Band, I am well aware of the strength of your presence. Thank you for giving your best to the project, as Austin City deserves.

My very special thanks go to Ric Jaz, Kenny Anderson, Brian Leach, David Service, Carolyn D. Roark, Jerry Tubb, and Dick Reeves for their commitment to this intensive work.

My endless gratitude to my mother Gulseren Nuhoglu, my wife, Irem, and my children, Eda and Ceyhun, for encouraging me to go after my dreams.

In my humble opinion, there is a lot of light, a lot of love, and a lot of joy in this story and music. I hope you enjoy it as much as I do.

Fehmi Nuhoglu, aka Franky

Made in the USA
Lexington, KY
16 March 2017